INCRETION

BRIAN STRANG

SPUYTEN DUYVIL

New York City

ISBN 0-9720662-3-3

Spuyten Duyvil, PO Box 1852 Cathedral Station, NYC 10025;
http://spuytenduyvil.net; 1-800-886-5304

Acknowledgements

I would like to thank the editors of *antennae* and *Volt* for
publishing poems from this book.

C O N T E N T S

…mankind has become a locustlike blight on the planet that will leave a bare cupboard for its own children—all the while in a kind of Addict's Dream of affluence, comfort, eternal progress—using the great achievements of science to produce software and swill.

—Gary Snyder, "Four Changes," 1969

gold teeth

the body eaters chisel

and seeds pound meaning

living is composed and

carves calamity in strata

turned against mosses

footsteps become unbearable

impulse to run

scratch a course

a blind enclosure and strangers

see self piercing window

above ambulating turn

into match stick heads

curved white walls chime with contact

discover cupped warmest

hand tongued imperatives

on sheets the gift changes features

on and on about the same things throw the door

in will come or out will move makes one pain hearing

scratches on the insides such small weeds

in stacks of paper flat tires cheerless lawn

arms found curled stick fingers

trails as a tail a human cocoon

within bundles form clutching

leather pouch for the trip to the stars

billowing of birds

eyes sewn shut with thin black hair

shows through the outer casing

burned them to hide their existence

the secrets seep from the ground

flashing on the surface

palms up asking for something

 helplessly alive and ignorant

they surround and part

before you as the breeze

just touch so as you pass

imagine such things

this curled form asks you

for nothing asks of you

under the strain

muscles ache do not respond

in the ground and above moving

faces that peel wrapped in burlap

through space under

the wind you can do nothing

fires that consume vocabulary

turn upon themselves

out snuffing marshes

lines on your hand and forehead

what one asks for

and sometimes gets

unknowable in the small hours

a rush toward the horizon

orange color rolls on the plane

of ocean the color

a physical presence

terrible admission of illusion

blind periscope

knocking bells

a great intelligence

bone spores

shrewd articulator

balances the short evening

prompts to action

underneath everything

The mind and the body race. A flash in the darkness signals presence. There are more signals. Panic suppressed. A sharp eye in the mirror, in the dark, a view down the hall. It is your movements you see. Realize you are seeing yourself.

A disorganization in the reeds: the man, athletic and in his prime, was hung by his neck.

The whole thing was kind of stupid. The remark is the clever and easy way out.

Make yourself into improvisation without rigor. Wonder how it will be sniffed out.

Something about the sincerity that is lost but easily disregarded. Nostalgic, the tones and sounds. But there was something possible and grand.

Brittle air, sheer lights, sheets of small twinklings filled the room with lanky legs, pomp and deception, a game of sorts. Cobalt and persimmon voluptuous interior, a stoned and lazy offer of sex on the couch. Into a sticky web of possibilities on the floor laughing. The potential of privilege.

You were on your way home late at night and in the dark, rural part of this flat terrain you saw a tall and gaunt man alone on the side of the road without a car and in a suit that was too small for him. You pulled over to ask the man if he would like a ride and the man nodded, said thank you barely opening his mouth, and got in. The man stared straight ahead into the darkness, into the road and the night and the blackness, his angular, hungry face floating in a pool of dashboard green. After more than an hour, he said this is where I get out, yawning out a deep laugh, revealing an entire set of gold teeth. When you slowed the car and pulled over to let him out, the man exited abruptly, slamming the door, disappearing into a country graveyard.

When you woke in the middle of the night and walked down the hall, you saw a figure disappear around the corner into the next room, just a quick brush of shoe and leg and you begin to wonder. You followed only to discover whether you were here and you look into the other room and see a family of four watching the television set. It was lonely they said and the kid was crazy too and they disappear and you hear some voices but they don't talk like children.

after such losses the moaning drives one

throughout the day heads hung on the benches

around the wall driven by the thought

by the scale of the games being played at their expense

as they continue to put one after the other below

the surface of understanding into

the tumbling heat and bones of crumbling walls

to cloying gray hands you fall through it into

the loss of fixed points of reference

sensing signs fly by

a mouth with fibrous teeth pulling inward

burlap under skin breaks open air

A storm is coming after some time. They head into the catacombs: a deal is struck in the elevator, a lizard eye and scaled foot, a quick handoff on a street corner, direct from the laboratory. In a brown bag: it could be someone's lunch. A sealed eye feels its way along, traces the cracks in the corridor, slams itself into its box, content to be closed and fed through a tube. Once inside, it grows to the proportions of its container. The air in the room is still and sick.

And in the villages, they fend for themselves with encoded elementals, seeds with terminal genes imbedded for dearth. A handful of dust and stunted dry weeds leaves one in serious doubt. In vast warehouses, rows of steel drums. Between them a gestation creeps over the surface, lodging itself in the cracks, making its own world push through the fibers around it. A helicopter fire flies around the perimeter, flashing its red tail.

Giving up the future and dear sleep. Staring at the vacant seat next to you in a cab ride.

A cold virulence: the actual event held just behind the iris.

A string of temptations. Holding to a place in the floor.

a science of models

The cracking of frozen water. Furrows exposing winged impression.
Chewing moths that were once dragons. Bodies whose story is that
of passing and who remain as a reminder, the complete loop of a cir-
cle. History from the layers.

Each is a book. Hold them in your hand and feel the blood through
the veins in your fingers. Nerve endings make contact with what is
there. A record of what is.

Look across the valley as you used to see it, as a place less laminat-
ed with construct. You are in contact with no one, holding onto a
flat encumbered wisdom deeper than your experience. New devel-
opments bristle across its surface. Its measure is that of the hillsides.
Spit onto the ground in front of you. Stop here and take measure-
ments.

You owe so much yet take the ground you stand upon for granted. Press your palms into the dust. This is an immovable silence. You collect some papers and stack them neatly in the field, trying for a semblance of order, falling asleep with a finger to your lips, thinking that this is a science of models.

Bodies stiffen preventing migration. Distribution channels prevent many from getting the food they'll need. What you think is thinking is really an intersection of slow-moving natural forces and the human toll of misery. You realize that time is a circle.

"I thought that if we were never separated the woods would never dry out, the air would never chill and water would never become scarce. I thought that we would remain here always, that mortality would remain an abstract concept, that we would hide in bed together as a birdman peered through the window."

Elms dig into the negative space of the horizon. An eye on the vine turns to sand and lanterns float in the stream. The roots thrust into the banks tearing against it.

And now the campaign of documents has begun, merciless even on the skin. This has nothing to do with silence. Deep bending movements of gaunt figures, outlines on the sand are pulling along a great wheel, making way for the leaders. Everything is calm here before the entrance, before their fingers move toward their faces and slender nails dig into lips.

You are totally free and continue deep inside the borders. The retaliation is only beginning and previous warnings were missed. You hope that they will stop passing resolutions. The measure of breath is the same as the thought that it produced. And now from this ancient mouth comes the sound of a piercing new language, a message of apocalypse, mechanization and indifference. And yet you know that this language is not new, that things turn to sand, that resolve is impermanent, that connections become tenuous.

In the streets of a forgotten city, dust clogging its arteries, overlaying its plan with time and uncovered in this city are a people who speak to us about what we have become and say that we are the same and yet we have ruined everything. The impact of this is heightened in the translation and we listen and yet we do not change and the row of elms has come down splintered and the banks of the rivers and lakes are wider than ever and the beach is littered with swollen dead fish. You had heard the town was beautiful and it was and there is only lament now when you see it.

lupus

A drama of failure plays itself out. Extraordinary difference and risk, an imaginary grid projected onto the city. Travel from place to place in search of food. A dimpled surface, a switchyard of mirrors, an eclipse and a magnifying glass on an achingly dark day. In a minute or two the body will be encased in molded plastic. Illumination in the ring, wowing the passive multitudes, saturating their limits, where everyone is chasing the balmy air. They will fan out and gorge on insects, adapted with exquisite senses, photographed in the night. The body will be hardened by morning.

Carnivores, pack-hunting remnant populations at the edge of rivers are at home in the lifeless statuary, in the will and power of an imperial landscape. Loping and devoid of individualism on the street, they edge toward restricted to the outskirts in their proliferation. They gobble up the land, slaughtering powerful hearts in the marketplace.

Candlelight casts an exact circle the length of consciousness. There are cracks in this paradox. You are a helpless passenger floating over the boiling mud. Ancestral tribes. The portals.

Let the wind through your ribcage and heart. Each moment is intact and towering. The lake, the bay, the ocean. On your forelegs, sip from a pool. The same existential view from any angle. Once every several years you are complete. Always the same with reverberations. Full of noises and presences. What is it called? The tension made you sit completely still. Made you alive by moving.

One figure in the foreground, another looking over the shoulder anticipating the excitement and violence to come. A row of trees on the avenue, a connection between strangers. You wouldn't believe it if it came to you. It is not really violence you realize, sharing a fear with someone you don't know. The shape of curiosity. A poison apology made to watch as it goes down into a shallow of eyes, a force of nature to work itself out. Blame it on family history, the great escape from this situation. Wonder why expenses run so high, just before you run out of the room. Make your way along the river again so high up in the air it flows and you fall down so low before yielding until you hold in your arms the reasons and jump into your car. Speed through a tunnel until the faces begin to swirl over your windshield through the guts of your being. They cloy.

Run back into your bedroom and look for an answer. And now on foot through the tunnel again, deaf to everything but the howls of tires and the echoes of a thousand more.

Shards of glass, wind and sun, a sunken body of strangers, individual humans face down on the ground, left arms tucked behind, right ones outstretched, pointing, claiming a place. Lined in a row, faces on the lawn, some kind of peace makes its way here even as radios blare. The soot crystals the face. The war dead hum and multiply.

So many of them go unrecognized, eased by the mud, drawing up to the surface of the earth. All of these open windows make them hard to avoid. The stream passes, a slippery line through the stillness. Dormant hollows; written history disappears, between the roots of trees. The prevailing disquiet is toward more physicality, movement that awakens to the fact of movement. And now they give way to the living, on the verge. Gazing into the avarice, coming to a boil, turning on themselves. These developments are the same as they have always been. The wolves are inside the city gates. It is raining and they have come to knock on doors.

An unbearable din. Humming warmth. And the air between here and the mountain ridge is orange in the waning light. You disintegrate into it. Empty river banks, approaching a fact of the day infringing on the outlines of the visible. Wavering ghosts unmake themselves. In the reeds, a movement assuring you of impermanence. A small cry more closely. A mosquito cloud feeds on the hovering remnants of the city.

indispensable

giants kick the heads off trees

twist and slither inside a dark candle

sucking poison from the air

quiescent names in reference bins

the moon and gravel stone under foot

something inside untroubled by memory

this mistake can be a life you might just see

an accumulation grinds you away

meet afield on the sign of the astrolabe

and take what is given

from the hanging vines

this world accords its own dimensions

someone you've never met has occupied

the house you left behind

watch them in the afternoon from afar

a bed on the ground

weep when your eyes are closed at night

celebrate the world in its passing

paranoia on all frequencies shouts about an other

outside the window along the highway

industrial parks and corporate retail complexes

collapsed and drugged fantasies

heavyweights packed into their soda cups

the difference in this elaborated sphere is looking

a matter of predation reeling under the sky

obsessed with islands of voices

the tapes running constantly

ordinary people in their offices

cultivated in laboratories on the burning floor

laughing through yellow glass

hoarding for the future for the day

after this one in the clearing outside of town

with tidy ideas in their shirtsleeves

an outpost is washed away

under pressure changeling skinny bodies

gather to watch themselves in their own show

where they can be uncovered

snip away the marks of observance

remain missions of theory

alight and unraveled like summer camps

the roads grow with the corruption of goods

in this tradition of planes and points

radio for help on a signal you cannot hear

from a century ago who could stop up rivers

in the long-sleeping solitude

on the poles are dead countries

under foot this thing crawls

smoking on the front drive of the complex

drop from branches as rotting orange shells

who became gelatinous before they passed

small city on a plate for you to eat

the tapes gather your every thought

wisdom of matter

This is a kind of tear in the fabric. You are among the pondering. They lean down into your capsule.

Remain unencumbered by eating and refusing at the same time, by giving credence to the transparent figures among the candlelight, by letting yourself feel the fear as you walk toward an open door. There is a needling aliveness on the palms of your hands and ridge of your neck. Look down and see that you have wheels under your feet.

You feel a deep sense of afternoon, facing the sun, and you wonder which houses are real. The body's own wisdom of matter questions the space you move through. And now you glide into an extension of the inconceivable, a vivid release of suffering.

There will be some big words afterwards—corruption, regeneration, geometry. But you are in the natural retreat of the season, flooded in innocence and forgetfulness, and you make your way back to your capsule, basking in the warm humanity of everything.

A split eye opens, trying not to become attached, not to feel like any-thing. It grows pushing upward like a tuber in its little hole, an unsatisfied creation in the beds. Running water pours over the sun and the brain. They are inconsequential in the light. Rub your hands together in the muck that it brings as it covers your skin and dries away your anger. See that what is in you is in everyone, that as they lie on the leaves around you, even as they chop each other down, you can sow yourself a new evening, even as the nights become longer.

Let yourself go into it. There is a table of scissors, a camera eye float-ing through the room. Understand why nobody will go into a room of red paint. Get out of this predicament and know that you've made a mistake. An accumulation of experience makes you grind a root between your teeth in annoyance. And someone you've never met hangs banners from the rails and watches them stir in the antiseptic wind. Before bed, remove the stones you carry in your shoes as you walk along the concrete shoreline.

You decide to listen to the sway of life around you. You think about the day you have had and ask whether you know prices better than species, whether the prices you know are fixed by a system, whether the trees in your neighborhood are fixed by a system, whether you are part of this. Are you water and ashes or crisp ink on a sheet of paper? Ask whether your hand wrinkles when you clench it or whether it is abstract and foolproof, an integer in your mind. Ask whether you bleed or multiply, subtract or desiccate, whether from the meat on your skeleton grow nutrients and mosses or interest and accruement, whether you join or separate, whether you are blood on the inside purpling away as part of the whole or inert and timeless carbon.

Birds fly away as you approach, making you into a small figure in the landscape. The sound you hear is that of grass blades rushing into the opening of your ears. This is the sound of many people and animals and plants over a long period of time. And the soil clutches loosely.

replacement

A species that learns to endure. People who cut holes through rock, who arrive with little fanfare, alkaline dust in the pores. A figure is on the horizon, the nearby hill soaked in red, hanging by the feet in individual freedom, leaving the people stretched, the graveyard of the nameless. A voice enters above the plain:

"This one is more than a shade with a cane, little ones. There is a whole history behind this fragile life. Though you hear me, you do not understand. There is history behind life. Though you hear me, you do not understand."

The seconds are pared to the moment when it will happen. Breathing is as quiet as possible. Carloads arrive, with men hiding their guns beneath their clothes, working the sweat through their hatbands.

You awake in a hotel far from your own, surprised anyone knows your name. You leave and meet someone at the market and have a brief conversation in a language not your own. You return to your room, find your clothes out of order, pour yourself a drink and stare out the window, making several telephone calls, mostly leaving messages. A park across the street has been torn up. Trees and chunks of asphalt now fill the space. You wonder what will be constructed. Something must always replace. You look out the window again and see a man on a side street struggling to open a briefcase with a knife and someone knocks on your door. No, you reply, maybe tomorrow. Something must always replace. You sit on the edge of the bed, noticing your pants rise slightly above your socks as you sit, wondering how long you will need to stay here.

In another room, a man feels he is a mental enthusiast. He demands founding myths, a meditation in the midst of violent shocks. On this earth, the scourge is unchained. He stares through the ceiling of his room. He practices sumptuous reflection and describes the images with piety. But those plagues are irreversible and soon everything considered will be imagined. The land slips under the sea and a foaming thunder of official documents can do nothing to stem the losses. Viruses mutate again and again and claim hundreds of thousands. He walks to the window, waiting for the contact to come. A rational shadow covers him and the waves break from left to right. Acrid surge of the world under pressure: the body pushes into it and feels a realism renewed by contact.

The natives have cut us off from the village, from the strip mall settlement. We have come into possession of our own lives and have come to start anew. And they want to kill us and they cannot be blamed for this. It is natural that we would collide. From raven-haired men, the secrets will be divulged and we will live on their blood, taking it to the center of our foundations. With difficulty we have avoided their arrows, though they will return, and for our momentary lapses, we will pay dearly, watering the ground with our spleen in the warmth of direct sunlight. Lesser things have spelled the end and the ends will come hidden in smiles. A genial narrative will follow and a chasm will open and leave us orphaned, clustered together in habitual anxiety.

ring of teeth

The lessons are replacing what brought them about. Everything threatens perspective, dimensionless and matte-gray. An all-powerful landscape takes us above the soil in a formless freedom, a uniform gesture convincing as heavy clay, an ample admission, stale as it is pragmatic at all points. To get out of poor beginnings what begins to dominate all of your senses. A foreign element has been introduced into your genetic makeup.

An immovable wilderness is pocked with attempts to dislodge it— what we cannot imagine delivers us. We watch dramatically as the new year brings a commotion, an orb that deepens memory.

Here there are grand hotels, armies of servants for the saints, and lilies grow from the dead. Ice shelves crack into the abyss. But the supermarkets are imbedded with arsenic and the cruelty of this calendar empire is stamped on our brows. And other more reversible problems burrow through the heart.

They were preoccupied with a game of moving tentacles, clumped around the source of their anxieties, a heat vent at the bottom of the ocean. Leeches are applied to our suffering. The wound bleeds and bleeds, a ring of shiny teeth sawing throughout the night.

And in the country, the hoppers are filled with prickly cotton and hateful slogans. Water falls on dried dust, making imprints the size of soldiers, no room for summer. A tongue approaching music, a cobbled hollow throat fills with venom. And the plans are solemn: thin transmitters beneath the skin. The streets are right and are true; a grid allows only the imaginable. The earth sinks in a gentle curve.

You know the answers: tremors from the hills, wire and speed, clones. Reminds you of an eye, of a time when you missed everything, of nuzzling fear and permeated memory itself: an undulating mass of conflict from this vantage point. This is a wheel of circumstances, a great movement, the sound of jets. The signals have reached you and the network has been established. Now your specific desires have turned on themselves and the land is consumed. No more room for small ones. It is as large as it is invisible.

empire

Most of our goods have been requisitioned and we build for the sake
of the emperor who loves to make war. Great stone heads are lifted
onto pedestals at the gates of the capital. We move among the pro-
posals and the destruction of argument itself, but are certain and per-
fectly comfortable and they do not represent our lives. We hear
reports of a group sponsoring attacks, though we know it will end
badly and we suspect that the rumors are not true. A point is made
for us and we do not understand what it means.

A vengeful antheap emerges, a zestful crawling in the territory. It
takes on all critics and lodges in the reasoning of tyrants. Absorption
occurs through the pores and crowds, complaining of the volume on
their headsets, gather around the relics. The years crawl over them
in the night, a choice for all to make. Something happens to each one
individually, against a backdrop painted to look like a city. People
worth more than the paper they are printed upon.

The heads on poles remind you that you walk on the same ground as your conquerors. But the pleasure of construction, of experimentation, of the senses stripped to their roots, is available to you even in this hostile environment. Break your shoulders free and move from within your skin and out of the top of your shell. There is a stone arch and scarcity on the streets. And on the shelves, a lot of bandages and tongues that lick and spurt. Spit the remains of an apple, for in this overwhelming stink of fear, in the circular caverns, the flashing lights and the messages from split lips, there are humane proportions somewhere. There is the clatter of eye contact. There is the gaudy collage of shared experience.

And in an orange-glassed imagination, a row of pebbles lines the
center of the floor. They are wishes. And behind the streaking
panes, the house creaks and gold doorknobs lead to the untouched.
Overhead, the dead eyes of the emperor mock them. A white heli-
copter. The air has melted. Late in the night, he moves on the water
and economies collapse in his wake. The pebbles grow in the morn-
ing light.

the flood

Through the back of the eye of someone else, the waves of pedantry: no one deserves a greeting or hello. See that this eye is bent, an astigmatism. Tone deaf and preaching to a room of white, they are in the middle, a barrage of transparent signs.

Some like this sort of thing. The wars remind them of privilege, make them feel bad and better now that they know they are exempt from destruction. Everyone you know is hiding beneath the ground. One day you will have a house and will enjoy electricity and vegetables will grow.

The sun dips into the eroded shoreline, the storms. One hundred thousand acres burn inland. The rivers fill the valley slowly. You hoped to never see the ocean change.

The young fill the halls with music and the tables are lined with food. When someone enters, they are subjected to questions: "Did you see her face?" It is hung from a silk kerchief, a remembrance permeated with collective desire. Troubled sleep and a naïve dream of peace, of everyone getting what they want. The waters flow. The house is lifted from its moorings. Come and sit at a table. Take your turn at the fountain.

Fresh sheets await in this motel. You bear the scars of someone who has been spreading a message of disintegration. And when these billions get what is owed to them, the house will settle back onto its foundation. And the river will come flowing through the windows. Hope for something, for deliverance. There is no reason to feel this way. Drive in your car to the outside of town, to a place where reading is done through the eyes of someone you know.

Someone owns all that you see. You remember a time when forests grew more than chin-high. The messenger lies bleeding at your feet.

The lungs of the earth burst from the surface and all is forgiven. In the putty skies they are dislodged. A sound like kids with bicycles taps along, comes apart at the seams. Placed over the spot is a black cloth, a mark of chalk on the face, circling in watchful presence. So rarely does anyone see the bicycles out in the open during the middle of the day. For safety's sake they avoid the letters and find a way to ask questions without them.

Out on the waves, the captain has lost his head. The plot is gone in the depth of it. You feel that this pack has come too close for your liking, has begun to nip at your heels.

This automaton that makes its way among the bones cannot be living. Yet you see it has a face and you know that your attachments make you whole but are your undoing as well. It is picking clipped wings. These are just parts of people, slices of personality, some very green. The workings of teeth, a death's head suspended in champagne bubbles. To some it is a mask or a moment of bliss, disconnected from the conflict that is sure to rise in its wake. The spindly ringing of spokes on the ground follows.

And in the tree lines on the shore you see flames, campfires of silver and mustard. Someone moves through the bushes. You see the flash of bicycles and you see that a hail of arrows is launched toward your ship and you know that this is to be expected, that this would be coming, that, while you hate them for it, they can not be condemned for this action.

You find that you are clutching possessively as always in the heat of things and that the captain, a dandy in red, has swum to shore and has become tangled in the vines. You know what awaits him.

Matter has gone up in the breeze, a night of lights, of grave silences, of silhouettes moving around a fire. These figures try to connect.

Move away from the favorite words toward a vacant hole in your language: something new has come into existence here.

A mote spins away through infinity. You are in a sinkhole, in a remnant of an ancient well, a language covering you, a bed of small hands leaving prints on your body. And, even if it were possible to change, you would have it no other way, seeing that this is a common condition. You lie on your back, completely still in the darkness, wondering whether you are facing the sky or the earth.

stamped

Nothing to you now. It turns into waste as you turn your back and measure what hasn't yet happened against what has. Into junk. Everything has come to be, an abundance hanging in rows, cars crashing outside your windows, the hoods crumpled into their windshields.

You are in desperate grounds now. Remember the bodies that scratched along the ground, how they ended in clichés of ancient societies, of spurs hanging from the rafters. Hold your body tall and move through the images whether they are real or not. You believe your existence depends upon it. They rest on a faulty premise, supported by mud on the backs of walking people. Construct is the antithesis of living.

Surrounded by trees as the only witnesses. Run along or walk but move through the cruelty, the demonstrations of relational power. The coastlines sink incrementally but visibly. Ask whether you have witnessed this or whether it is without you. Roll up your limbs.

Wanting nothing but to work, opening sight in the fabric, a reminder around your neck, weighing you down, you want to make it worthwhile. On a sea full of life, you find that individuals burn in memory only a short while. Not even your own hands. Yourself into the wall itself, an arm protruding. Visit the sites where the sky becomes bricks. An asphalt parking lot. Swallow hard and lose yourself in the region.

There seem to be only the shadows here. And we believe in them and are guided by them even as we take them so casually, as we drive on their freeways, speak into boxes at the gates and we trace the three billion names on our spines. And deep in the laboratories, they stamp themselves into our codes. If you look closely, you will see their trademark: the seeping chambers of a volcano, the false dawns of clinical treatment, organs and embryos for implantation.

Most move several feet off of the ground over great distances at great speeds to their screens. And they mock, assuring themselves that the images have no effect and we can control and frequent the places made for us in a world stamped deeply into the earth's fabric, spinning through space at a slightly slowed rate.

And in some remote parts, they turn from the screens and into vegetal forms, wriggling and aging, covered with birds that peck through to the soft parts, the exoskeletal encumbrances. They heave and spit, sensitive to the resistant strains. They look for ways to ask the questions, wondering and looking for where… The question is not-yet-formed. It hovers at the racetracks, stadiums, theaters and all public places, dripping beneath the seats.

And now you begin to wonder whether the emergence of your relative values was a great mistake, whether you'll allow yourself the life raft of universals, whether you really have a choice and whether you think your carefully-crafted self image is one of encumbrance, the soft parts of a weighty carcass. Or is the ground made of husks? Do you lie among the needles and cones, mask your face hoping that no one will notice you, that the smell of your hide will not attract nocturnal predators and you hide in your room undermining all of the great minds and saying some things that are true.

But stupidity falls like rain and power turns people into jackals, turns those without it onto the roads, gnawing on the bones of rodents, begging for scraps from bored faces behind glass.

The theorists have lost what is underneath—a smooth cobalt orb with very few defenses, cracking apart at the poles.

There is something of action and circumstance in these gestures. One cannot forget from where they come. Where did you disappear to? In the woods you were running across simplicity and were ensnared in a web of complexity. And now you cannot find reason for conversation nor for the principles on which it relies.

And the rain begins to turn and everyone is throwing tantrums against the flat sky and temperature-controlled air which shakes only by your movement through it, excluding you as a member of this system. You want too much, to be even a small part of the world.

On a green lake, you throw stones which stick to the surface. You are in a dizzying moment of circumstance and must find yourself subject to the illnesses and wonders of your class. You wander about again, down the streets, in the burning real. In the burning present, whisper that you remember our tragedies as the knife sinks deep. And you crawl back under the water, the primordial synaesthesia, the ebb and flow. And you watch the frost melt from the edge of the world.

T H E   N U M B E R S

number nine

it is all a problem all of it going on going

under but where there is no problem there is little

so problems are the only state

which make up the constant figuring

take in the facts as they appear as people are

skinned to basics to bones just like

you get into the last stages you look for

connection through the eyes hoping

that these are not the last parts through a door

at the end of a pier off into the dark water out farther

than you would dare to swim nothing can come

of the arms over the rails when the water

never reaches this high and walk through the bottomless

dark of this door with a false cherry taste in your mouth

on a bed of reflected yellow lights and blue white stars

decide which of these you will call fish at all

number eight

starting again from a new point with no control

at all over the forces around you

ponderous faces leaning into your capsule a kind of tear

in the fabric of your daily existence find some place

natural to you take in the facts as they are see that behind

the faces are people skinned to their bones just like yours

as we approach the final stages look for connection

with others in the eyes hoping to find someone just like

that white clapboard in the sun and a billowing tree

monuments of cedars and ponderosas or

tiled roofs the shine of streetcar tracks work

alone a fiction has entered but lies on the bricks gasps

barely mentioning the uprooted chances and you will not let

yourself rise in a bubble of greed or fall in a weary cascade

of sundowns or be sunken to the ocean's bottom wrapped

in a tangle of obsession and chides remain so unencumbered

and ask that your lot be spared by eating and refusing to eat

by giving credence to the transparent figures among

the candlelight of your living space by feeling the fear

walk toward the open door

needling aliveness over your skin you will not

move sideways vine-entangled bones loosen

number seven

filling your world with everything

a sword has run through

unable to find living victims

bless this thing in front of you

in the presence of an eternal presence in these stones

never in the many years of my own animation

hands holding each others' remains

how can there be anything I haven't told?

something has given way

at the shock of the phone call

the most impossible connection

better off not using the door

part of you is sleeping in a chair for so many years

a deeply disturbed trance but you can not wake

and if you were to

it would not be waking

you are outside the glass

facing yourself on the inside

the most artificial distances between

across a small room with so much floor

number six

one can find stacks of it on the shelves but

none are as daring

and a new point has been realized always a new point

is being reached history is a stack of papers and they

are always most correct at the present an accumulation

of new points of riddles and unsolvable questions and

always most right right now toward a point of outpouring

an awakening to the moment of its occurrence

a mark of in-between-ness confusion is rich water

but the loss of history and movement bring about

a stagnant pool of the self without connection

without a web of growth and influence

questions and parts of your life you had forgotten

accumulate more than a premise verge on your sphere

you swing the axe felling what is in your way

but it grows despite you again after you have gone

a kind of meditation only to have this time here

to recognize it when it is gone only to see it

at the moment of its occurrence until it becomes you

and you are washed clean from its core with the next rain

and a great moth overhead burns itself in the sky falling

fertile ashes and fearful drones surround its fall and point

and shake their heads until they fall from airplanes

one through the windshield of a car

number five

without pretense eating together and laughing

a thin line with the day cleaving the hide and bone

stories that end teething ice cubes trying to ignore the deaths

for a few hours the munitions at the bottom of the sea

eat our way out of this mess for now

low rents and drinks around a table

eyes droop with satisfaction with the stories

there is no buildup the punchline comes as all others

until you realize it is there as all others just a funny fact

that is something no one can figure out

number four

you are alone in a garden melting your divine nerves

in the hour for sleep wrinkled and drenched tongue

pink with embers and silk stockings waving in the wind

walk home in naïve eagerness a crowd of fidelity and chaos

and heavily policed dawn climbs hand over foot on the

 supernatural: a night made into a mute fathomless pool

look for prey in the water arms dangling incubated eggs

living beings with white wings advancing on the street

but a factual dawn sows truths more true

a period of transformation is under way

an amphibian school for the rest of life a likeness

to make plain what is and has been

botched plots with nobody present

reflection in a forbidden turbulent eddy

number three

you wonder where this napkin has come from

sitting in your lap not what it used to be

around you how it is connected as you look out

the office window through distant trees as you stare

through multiple panes of glass through the clamor

in herbal infusions and caffeine-free purgatory

an intermission in the open field and you

rest your head supported by sheathed hands

little time for preparation

a prolific silence living on the inside

in the parking lot the stories need a reinterpretation

the same story when you do something for yourself

later in your life you will know already how it ends

when we are brought down there is the storm

for all to see the man who killed his kin who released

a box of demons where they were singing songs clutching

the rich earth grows up through your feet becomes sinuous

and flaking away just enough for sustenance the sound

of animal digestion through the soles of your feet

the structure giving way on unstable shale

glowing faces that laugh through their food

and you too sit and shrill in the cold air

fields still in your lungs wrenching inverted branches

sputter out loose breakage cheer goes on and later

you are in smoke and sound fires wooden bowls of burning

a heap in the center of the room you were so ill-formed then

this very conversation would have terrified you so that

made you panic away pull the roots of the people you know

of this very field and lie beneath the frost to speak of

there is a nervous man shaved of his ears standing

in the door across the field in sight reminds that these

thoughts have stayed for days wearing your clothes

hanging around eating you a prescience a voice grown close

and monotone with age now standing and speaking in front

of you a girl in a night dress with mud on her hands

and this man was walking across the grass as you lie

on your belly as you were as you are going about your life

tried to comprehend that every person you pass has a whole

life as you try to fathom that every car has at least one

that nothing you say is even close to the complexity

concrete by working on concrete thoughts as thoughts can

not be even a discarded straw the fronts of buildings a car

door a bell an iron gate matches scrap of paper leaves

spilled oil paint mud a plastic lid not even a stack of books a cogent infant looking side to side in the new land

coat hanger several hooks an immense society plastic bags

number one

of encounters and echoes and outlaws comes

undone the scratched markers in any city anywhere

immediately into a morbid streak of words

faces are shadowed by newly-enacted regulations

gone wrong somehow one can tell no time here

of greatcoats in coherence behind the doors

dragonfly in its component parts

the cracks in the sidewalk as guides

no good laughed the buttons on your shirt

the happy stance a forest of eyes

in and out of sleep on the edge of a highway

drift into traffic hit the lines and drift back

throughout the day they can be overwhelmed at sunset

as the conditions allow assimilation as a faucet running

to touch the cards to arrange alphabetically

the kind of personality created by newspapers

into loose shredded cotton figures slumping

the victory and delirium closes in on a small circle

a handful of stems from some nearby carcass the facts

make themselves present in things but things change

as may become the circumstances of the day as one defines

a day or each moment going on and on in the same way

as curled branches stretch with trails of skin

beetle ticking off seconds at the pace

the rivers and seas
—for elisa

64

a kind of action and

    consequence undone

        where granular

            watch the ritual

                watch the buildings

                    collapse the air heating

in lincolns and biscaynes

    making the world round

        fat-bellied can crushers

            sky flashes skeleton wings

                the emperor's daughter

                    guts them where they lie

from the window

    tumescent men

        the gum chewers

            in the great room

                flap their wings

                    to launch

from the pool bar

    cocktails in the moonlight

        and the night radiation

            a population killing itself off

                they are in the final stages

                    are bathing beauties

and this area holds

    a chlorinated life

        strips vegetation

            your head will burn

                despite the worst intentions

                    as the winds begin to beg

life forms overturned

a thick-skinned reptile

closes its docile eyes

as the rain from the eaves

he mirrored lagoon

even as the skies

a gallows darkness

deathly yellow

on the surface

your feet through loam

as the boat drifts away

in this shallow sea

field of burning crabs

in their mud holes

in the balance

of destruction

the waters cut off

crashing through

trash bleached

    between the bones

        spindly planes

            transport exposed

                the walking roots of trees

                    a stadium of skins

we are now in the center

    of the entire world

        hidden from the wings

            of the fisher kings

                a roaring machinery

                    the underside of water

into hearts into cities

    storm-shocked eye

        the cut grass overrun

            an amoebae a tadpole

                blue bloated fauna

                    waves right themselves

pull up the darkness

    a thick chain net

        apparitions toast

            when rivers run backward

                the memory of fishers

                    screened porch ghosts

walkers without feet

    and life bleeds and rises

        through the mud and eyes

            insistent teeming it

                petals and covers

                    everywhere around

insides

you will not find a space alive here

by the water the trains carrying

material look toward what

switches the weather permanently

fluids alone spreading

house plans cement themselves

oil across waves turbid

horizons unoriginal

only a few centuries will come

buds up and down vision

to your senses inside little factories

plungers drain and hollow

one with a machine moves faster

the parallels folding you

internal galleries

say that this is no life to live

for (anyone) to (live) this life

oscillation dilation cheers

injection inside insides

middle courses merry into the night

what has been implanted?

what has been absorbed?

what is automatic?

what has been assimilated?

you as leader of yourself

now the previous precious

night here a loss of solipsism

lean hard into muckery

is it too late?

are the changes irreversible?

does the problem have solutions?

what will be the results?

penchant for disaster

implantation in the neck

scanned in any public place

without touching skin

trading for the self the verge

effortlessly more extreme

peering through cracks

implosion in the soft blades